The Floating Orchard

Troon Harrison

Paintings by

Miranda Jones

Tundra Books

Published in Canada by Tundra Books, *McClelland & Stewart
Young Readers*, 481 University Avenue, Toronto, Ontario M5G 2E9

Published in the United States by Tundra Books of Northern
New York, P.O. Box 1030, Plattsburgh, New York 12901

Library of Congress Catalog Number: 00-131209

Canadian Cataloguing in Publication Data

Harrison, Troon, 1958–
    The floating orchard

ISBN 0-88776-439-8

I. Jones, Miranda, 1955– . II. Title.

PS8565.A6587F56 2000   jC813'.54   C00-930416-9
PZ7.H37Fl 2000

We acknowledge the support of the Canada Council for the
Arts and the Ontario Arts Council for our publishing program.

We acknowledge the financial support of the Government of
Canada through the Book Publishing Industry Development
Program for our publishing activities.

Medium: oil on paper

Printed and bound in Hong Kong, China

1 2 3 4 5 6   05 04 03 02 01 00

For my lovely sister, Gwedhen

T.H.

To Mum and Dad and the orchard I left behind

M.J.

Damson lived in the house her great-grandfather had built. Once every year she filled the pantry with jars of plum jam, and painted the shutters blue. "This is where I was born and where I will always live," she liked to say happily.

Around the house grew an orchard where a rooster and hens strutted, and sheep bleated. In spring the fragrance

of blossoms filled every room. In fall people came from
miles around to fill baskets with soft, sweet plums.

Damson's great-grandmother had planted the first plum tree in the valley. She brought the plum stone from far away, across an ocean, and said that it was magical. No one believed stories like that anymore, but the oldest tree stood tall and straight among the others. Damson called it the Orchard Queen, and took special care of it. She watered it on the hottest days of summer, and pruned it very gently.

Damson decided she must build a boat. In the woodshed she hammered and sawed, working as fast as she could, while the sheep sheltered in the doorway. On the third day of rain, water rippled among the plum trees. On the fifth day, water lapped at the doorway. Damson's boat was finished except for a mast. She laid down her tools and looked outside.

A man was in the orchard. Rain dripped from his hat and, when he saw Damson, he waved and splashed to the woodshed.

"You look cold and wet, stranger," she said.

"My name is Bartlett," he replied. "I have climbed many hills and crossed many valleys, planting pear seeds everywhere I go. Now I am far from home and have only one seed left. I'm trying to escape from this flood."

"I have built a boat," said Damson, "and you are welcome to ride in it. All it needs is a mast."

"For that we must have the trunk of a tall, straight tree," said Bartlett, and he waded into the orchard to find one. Water tugged at Damson's boots as she followed.

"This is the one we need," Bartlett said, standing below the Orchard Queen.

"No!" protested Damson. "This is a special tree. It grew from the first plum stone my grandmother planted in the valley."

"It is the tallest and straightest," Bartlett responded. "It is just right for a mast."

Damson knew that this was true.

The ax made a dull ringing sound as Bartlett chopped down the Orchard Queen.

Rain fell like tears on Damson's face.

There came a time when the wind blew cold
and the bees were silent. In the orchard the buds
were as tight as fists. One evening it began to
rain. All night water roared across Damson's roof.
All next day rain beat against her windows.
The creek overflowed its banks; muddy water
swirled to the orchard gate. The rooster and hens
huddled in the dripping trees.

We are going to have a flood, worried Damson.
What will happen to us all?

"This tree will be with us wherever we sail," Bartlett comforted Damson and, carefully, using his penknife, he carved a name on the boat. When the water was very deep, Damson hoisted the bright quilt sail and the *Orchard Queen* drifted away. The rooster and the hens huddled among the jars of plum jam and bales of hay. The sheep and lambs bleated mournfully.

Damson and Bartlett sailed down the valley,
among the highest twigs of the plum trees, and away
over the hills. They sailed for days and days, getting
farther and farther from home, passing empty barns

and floating among gardens. Damson had never traveled
so far and even Bartlett didn't know where they were.

"We will never find our way back, and all the blossoms
on my plum trees will be dead," said Damson sadly.

At last one morning the rain stopped. Sunshine was pale in the mist.

"Look!" Bartlett cried, pointing at a rainbow as bright as their sail. Trees and hills poked from the ripples. Beneath the *Orchard Queen* the water grew shallower until finally the boat ran aground on a hill. The sheep jumped out happily and began to eat the green grass. The rooster crowed in triumph and a hen laid an egg among the empty jam jars. Bartlett made a tent from the sail and began to explore.

Only Damson was sad. She missed her great-grandfather's house. She remembered how the plum trees had been hung with stars on winter nights. As she stroked the smooth mast, she began to cry. Her salty tears soaked into the wood. At the very tip of the mast, something strange began to happen.

M. Jones.

The old tree trunk put out
a bud. The bud opened into a
green leaf. Another leaf grew beside it.
"Bartlett!" shouted Damson. "Come and
see the mast!" In amazement they watched as
small twigs appeared, covered with green leaves.
"My great-grandmother was right," Damson
whispered joyfully. "The plum stone that grew
into this tree was magic."

"We must plant the mast on the hill,"
said Bartlett. "And I will plant my last pear
seed nearby."

They dug a hole and lifted the mast into it.
As it touched the wet earth it grew flower buds,
which opened quickly, like fingers unfolding.
The tree stood white and fragrant in the sunset.

By morning the tree was weighed down with soft, sweet plums. Damson and Bartlett picked them and planted their stones all over the hillside. An orchard sprang up, the slender young trees bending in the wind

as their blossoms opened. Beside the orchard Damson
and Bartlett built a house with blue shutters. Every summer
they filled the pantry with jars of plum jam, and people
came from miles around to pick fruit.

Damson's daughter was born at blossom time, and named Anjou Victoria. When she was small, she liked to chase the lambs among the dandelions. As she grew older, she took special care of the two tall, straight trees in the center of the orchard. One was the Orchard Queen, the other a stately pear tree.

Sitting in their shade with her friends, Anjou Victoria liked to say happily, "This is where I was born and where I will always live." She didn't know yet that life is full of surprises.